Bad Rap

by Nancy Krulik • illustrated by John & Wendy

Grosset & Dunlap

For the kids at the Rodeph Sholom Day School.
Thanks for the inspiration—N.K.

To Shane, a most rocking and
talented friend—J&W

 Published by Grosset & Dunlap, a division of Penguin Young Readers Group, 345 Hudson Street, New York, New York, 10014. GROSSET & DUNLAP is a trademark of Penguin Random House LLC.
Manufactured in China

Library of Congress Cataloging-in-Publication Data

Krulik, Nancy E.

Bad rap / by Nancy Krulik ; illustrated by John & Wendy.

p. cm. — (Katie Kazoo, switcheroo ; 16)
Summary: When Katie and Suzanne learn that their favorite band the Bayside Boys, will perform in Cherrydale, they think their biggest problem is how to get tickets, but Katie magically turns into one of the Boys and causes the band to break up.
ISBN 0-448-43741-4 (pbk.)
[1. Bands (Music)—Fiction. 2. Magic—Fiction.] I. John & Wendy. II. Title.
PZ7.K9416Bad 2005
[Fic]—dc22 2004017661

10 9 8 7 6 5 4 3 2 1

Proprietary ISBN 978-1-101-95136-1
Part of Boxed Set, ISBN 978-1-101-95128-6

Chapter 1

"And I dream of you when I awake!" Suzanne Lock sang out wildly as she danced around her friend Katie Carew's room.

"When I awake," Katie joined in, using her hairbrush like a microphone.

Katie's cocker spaniel, Pepper, howled loudly. Katie giggled. "That's it, Pepper, sing along!"

"That was 'Dreams' by the Bayside Boys," Joey G., the radio DJ, announced as the song came to an end. "Thanks for spending your Sunday afternoon with me, Joey G., on Cherrydale's number-one radio station."

"I think 'Dreams' is my favorite Bayside

Boys song," Suzanne told Katie. She flopped down onto the bed and tried to catch her breath.

"I love *every* song on their CD. It's like they're singing just to me," Katie sighed.

"Hey, that rhymes!" Suzanne exclaimed. "You sound just like T-Jon!"

Katie smiled. T-Jon did all the raps on the Bayside Boys' songs. He was so awesome. Suzanne had given her a real compliment!

"I can't decide which of the Bayside Boys I like the best," Suzanne said. She looked up at the poster on Katie's bedroom wall. "I mean, Fizzy's got that amazing braided hair. And T-Jon dances really well. And I love his sunglasses. But when Ace sings, I get all tingly. I'm glad he's the lead singer."

Katie shrugged. "I like Spike the best. He seems really nice. And I like the way he spikes his hair up in the front."

Suzanne laughed. "That's just like you, Katie. Hardly *anybody* likes Spike the best."

Bayside Boys

"That's okay," Katie told her. "I think he's cool."

"Sure he is," Suzanne agreed. "*All* the Bayside Boys are cool."

"I've got a special surprise for all you Bayside Boys fans out there!" Joey G. suddenly announced.

Instantly, Katie and Suzanne stopped talking. They stared anxiously at the radio.

"The Bayside Boys are coming to Cherrydale!" the DJ said.

"AHHHHH!" Suzanne screamed. "Dreams do come true!"

"Shhhh!" Katie told her. "We have to find out when!"

Suzanne quieted down.

"Ace, Fizzy, Spike, and T-Jon will be at the Cherrydale Arena this Saturday night to tape a cable TV special. Tickets will go on sale tomorrow morning at nine a.m.—but only at the arena's box office. You've got to be there in person to score your seats."

"Oh, wow!" Suzanne exclaimed. "Katie, we *have* to get tickets for that show."

"We can't," Katie told her sadly.

"What? Are you crazy? Of course we can. I have allowance money saved up," said Suzanne.

"So do I," said Katie. "But money isn't the problem."

"Then what is?" Suzanne asked her.

"Tomorrow is *Monday*," Katie reminded her best friend. "We'll be in *school* at nine o'clock."

Tears welled in Suzanne's eyes. "You're right. This is awful . . ." She brightened suddenly. "Unless . . ."

"Unless what?" Katie asked excitedly.

"Unless *your* mom can get the tickets for us. *She* doesn't go to school."

"That's true," Katie agreed. "Let's go ask her."

The girls raced down the stairs at top speed. Pepper ran after them, barking loudly at their heels.

"MOMMMMM!" Katie shouted. "I need you!"

"It's an emergency," Suzanne added.

Mrs. Carew came running out of the kitchen. "What's wrong, girls?" she asked nervously.

"The Bayside Boys are coming to Cherrydale," Suzanne blurted out.

"But we'll be in school tomorrow morning when the tickets go on sale," Katie explained.

"They're going to sell out," Suzanne said.

"You have to go and get tickets for us," the girls finished together.

Mrs. Carew took a deep breath. "Oh," she said. "Is that all?"

"Is that *all*?" Suzanne gasped. "Mrs. Carew, this is the most important thing that's ever happened to us."

Katie's mother laughed.

"Mom, tickets go on sale tomorrow morning at nine o'clock. Can you stop at the Cherrydale Arena and buy them for us?"

Mrs. Carew shook her head. "Sorry, girls. I have to be at work early tomorrow morning. I won't have time to get the tickets."

"How about Dad?" Katie asked hopefully.

"He's working, too," Mrs. Carew reminded Katie.

Suzanne thought for a moment. "My dad's out of town. But my mom will be around. We can ask her to get the tickets." She raced for the door.

"Where are you going?" Katie asked her.

"Home. I have to talk to my mom!" Suzanne exclaimed.

"Why don't you just call her from here?" Katie asked.

Suzanne shook her head. "This is a *big* favor. I want to ask her in person."

X X X

Ten minutes later, Katie's phone rang.

"I'll get it," Katie shouted, hoping it was Suzanne.

"Hello?" Katie said into the phone.

It was Suzanne. And she didn't sound happy.

"My mom has to take Heather to some dumb old baby music class," Suzanne told Katie angrily. "She didn't think getting tickets for the Bayside Boys concert was an important enough reason for her to miss it."

"But it *is* important," Katie said. "*So* important."

"I know that, and you know that," Suzanne sighed. "But my *mom* doesn't know that. I can't believe the Bayside Boys are going to be right here in Cherrydale and we won't get to see them. It's just not fair!"

Katie and Suzanne stayed on the phone for a little while, but neither girl said much. There wasn't anything *to* say. The fact was, they weren't going to the Bayside Boys concert.

And that really stunk!

Chapter 2

The next morning on the playground, everyone was talking about the Bayside Boys concert.

"I can't believe my mom wouldn't let me miss school to go get tickets," Jessica Haynes moaned.

"I know what you mean," Zoe Canter agreed. "This is so sad."

"Even my big sister Lacey wants to go to that concert," Emma Weber said. "But she's got a math test this morning. There's no way my parents would let her miss that to go buy tickets."

Katie sighed. "I really wanted to see the

Bayside Boys up close, especially Spike."

"It's just plain dumb," Suzanne told the girls.

"What is?" Katie asked her.

"It's dumb that the tickets went on sale today. All the Bayside Boys' fans are kids. And kids are in school on Monday mornings," Suzanne explained.

"Hey, that's right!" Mandy Banks exclaimed. "You know, I bet the concert won't sell out. At least not this morning!"

Katie's face brightened. "That means we can go get tickets *after* school."

"I was thinking the same thing!" Suzanne agreed. "Meet me here after your band practice."

"Okay, but I have to go back to my class-room and sign out with Mr. Guthrie before I can go home," Katie reminded her.

"That's all right," Suzanne said. "But hurry! We don't want to miss out on getting tickets!"

Katie turned to Emma W. “Do you want to come with us?” she asked, not wanting to leave her new friend out.

Emma frowned. “I can’t. It’s my turn to help my mom with the twins this afternoon.”

"Oh," Katie replied. "That's too bad. But maybe . . ."

Before Katie could finish her sentence, Becky Stern came running onto the playground. Well, not running, actually. She was doing cartwheels across the yard!

"Hey, everyone!" Becky greeted the girls as she landed right beside them. "I have the best news!"

"We already know," Suzanne told her. "The Bayside Boys are coming to Cherrydale. Katie and I are going to buy tickets this afternoon."

"Forget it," Becky told her. "They'll be sold out by then. There are already a thousand people lined up outside the Cherrydale Arena waiting for the ticket booth to open. I heard it on the news."

Katie frowned. *So much for great ideas.*

"If the show's going to sell out, why are you so happy?" Emma W. asked Becky.

Becky smiled. "Because *I* already have my tickets," she told her.

"That's impossible!" Suzanne exclaimed. "They don't go on sale for another twenty minutes!"

"I didn't *buy* my tickets," Becky boasted. "I got them for free."

"How did you do that?" Zoe Canter asked.

"The Bayside Boys record all their CDs at a studio in Atlanta. My dad used to play golf with the man who owns the studio," Becky bragged in her soft, Southern accent. "My dad's friend can get tickets to any Bayside Boys show he wants. He promised me two tickets to the show."

"Wow," Jessica said. "You're so lucky."

"*Two* tickets?" Suzanne piped up curiously. "Who are you taking to the show with you?"

Becky shrugged. "I haven't decided yet," she told her. She smiled. "It could be anyone." Then she turned and walked away.

Suzanne's eyes got very small. Katie could tell she was angry. "It could be anyone," she said, imitating Becky's accent. "Oooh. Blechy Becky is such a snob."

"You're just jealous, Suzanne," Mandy said.

"No, I'm not," Suzanne told her. "Why would I be? Katie and I are going to get tickets to that show, too."

"We are?" Katie asked her, surprised. "How are we going to do that?"

"I don't know yet," Suzanne said. She watched as Becky stopped to tell some of the other girls about her tickets. "But we will. We *have* to."

Chapter 3

As Katie walked into class 4A, she was wondering what plan Suzanne had for getting tickets to the concert. But she didn't have much time to think about that. There was a bigger question waiting for her in the classroom.

In fact, there were *lots* of questions waiting for the kids as they entered the classroom. Katie's teacher, Mr. Guthrie, had decorated the whole room with cardboard question marks. They were hanging from the ceiling, stuck to the walls, and on all the classroom windows. There was even a big question mark over Slinky the snake's cage.

"What's this all about?" Kadeem Carter asked Mr. Guthrie.

"Not *what*," Mr. Guthrie told him mysteriously. "Who."

"What?" Kadeem asked again.

"Who," Mr. Guthrie repeated.

Huh? Katie was getting confused!

Mr. Guthrie smiled at his class. "Take your seats, everyone. We're about to start a new learning adventure!"

Katie smiled. Most teachers would just say that the class was starting a new unit. But not Mr. Guthrie. He thought of learning as a big adventure. Emma W. and Katie moved their beanbag chairs next to each other and sat down. All the kids in class 4A sat in beanbag chairs. Mr. Guthrie thought kids learned better when they were comfortable.

"What do you think Mr. G. is up to this time?" Emma W. whispered to Katie.

"It could be anything," Katie told her.

The kids didn't have to wait long to find

out. Just then, Mr. Guthrie stood up and wrote three words on the blackboard.

WHO AM I?

George Brennan raised his hand high. "Finally, a question I can answer," he joked. "You're Mr. Guthrie."

"Correct," Mr. Guthrie laughed. "But actually, *Who Am I?* is the name of your new assignment."

Now *everyone* in the class was confused.

"Let me explain," Mr. Guthrie said. "Each of you will pick a famous person to research. Then, in two weeks, you will give an oral report, pretending to be that person. You have to dress up like him or her. And when you talk, you should try to sound like that person. Try to use some quotes that the person you choose actually said. Then the rest of the class will have to guess who you are."

"Do we have to pick a person from history? Can it be a movie star or an athlete?" Mandy Banks asked.

“You can choose anyone you want—as long as there’s enough information on that person for you to do your report,” Mr. Guthrie told her.

“I know just who I want to be!” George

exclaimed. "I want to be . . ."

"Don't tell," Mr. Guthrie said, holding up his hand. "That'll ruin the guessing part of the report."

"This is so cool," Kevin Camilleri said.

Katie didn't think it was so cool. She didn't want to become anyone else. Not even for a report.

That was because Katie knew better than anyone what it was like to become somebody else. She'd done that too many times already.

It had all started one day at the beginning of third grade. Katie had lost the football game for her team, ruined her favorite pair of pants, and let out a big burp in front of the whole class. It was the worst day of Katie's life. That night, Katie had wished she could be anyone but herself.

There must have been a shooting star overhead when she made that wish, because the very next day the magic wind came.

The magic wind was a wild tornado that

blew just around Katie. It was so powerful that every time it came, it turned her into somebody else! Katie never knew when the wind would arrive. But whenever it did, her whole world was turned upside down . . . switcheroo!

The first time the magic wind came, it turned Katie into Speedy, class 3A's hamster! It was pretty bad having nothing but chew sticks and hamster food to eat all morning. Luckily, the magic wind came and turned Katie back into herself in time for lunch.

The magic wind came back again and again after that. It turned Katie into all sorts of people—Mr. Kane, the school principal; Genie the Meanie, her camp counselor; and Mr. Starkey, her band teacher! Once, it even turned Katie into her old teacher Mrs. Derkman. Katie had come very close to having to kiss Mrs. Derkman's big, hairy husband, Freddy Bear. How gross would *that* have been?

The wind had also changed Katie into other kids—like Becky, Emma W., and Suzanne. Being Suzanne had been really bad. Katie had turned into her right in the middle of Suzanne's modeling show. Katie was *no* model. It had been a disaster.

Then there was the time the magic wind had changed Katie into her dog, Pepper. She'd spent the afternoon peeing on fire hydrants and eating a half-chewed bagel right off the sidewalk. Then this mean squirrel started throwing acorns at her head. After that, Katie decided that a dog's life wasn't as easy as people thought.

Being somebody else caused Katie nothing but trouble. That was why she definitely didn't want to do this *Who Am I?* project. But she couldn't tell Mr. Guthrie that. Not without explaining about the magic wind. And she didn't think Mr. G. would believe her. Katie wouldn't have believed it, either, if it didn't keep happening to her.

So Katie was going to have to pick a person for her project. But who? She glanced into her backpack. The book she was reading was right on top. It was called *Aesop's Fables.*

Hmmm . . . Katie really liked the stories in the book. But she didn't know much about Aesop himself. All it said on the book jacket was that he was an author who had lived thousands of years ago in Greece.

Katie thought for a moment. Since being a writer was on her list of things she might want to be when she grew up, it might be fun to learn about a writer who was as famous as Aesop.

Katie just hoped the magic wind never turned her into Aesop. She didn't want to live in a time when there were no TVs, stereos, or Bayside Boys concerts!

Chapter 4

As soon as school was over, Katie grabbed her book bag and her clarinet and raced to the playground. Suzanne was waiting for her.

"Do you want to come to my house, or should I go to yours?" Suzanne asked her.

Katie shook her head. "I can't hang out after school today. Mr. G. just assigned us a really big project."

"*Project?*" Suzanne exclaimed. "How can you think about schoolwork at a time like this?"

"A time like what?" Katie asked.

"A time when the Bayside Boys are coming to Cherrydale, and we're not going to be there!" Suzanne exclaimed. "We have to figure out a way to get tickets!"

Katie shrugged. "I don't think there's anything we can do about it. The concert's sold out. None of us will get to go."

"Except Becky," Suzanne said, making a face. "*You* don't have to sit in class and listen to Blechy Becky go on and on about having two tickets to the show."

Katie nodded. Becky was in class 4B with Suzanne. It must have been hard to hear Becky bragging about her tickets all day.

"And get this," Suzanne continued. "She's having a contest to see who will get the other ticket."

"A contest?" Katie asked. "What kind of contest?"

"She's making up a test with questions about the Bayside Boys," Suzanne explained. "Whoever answers the most questions correctly will get the ticket."

Just then Jeremy Fox, Katie's other best

friend, walked out into the schoolyard.

"Hi, Jeremy," Katie greeted him.

"Hi," Jeremy replied. "That was a good band practice today, huh?"

Katie nodded. She and Jeremy were both in the beginning band at school. Katie played clarinet and Jeremy played the drums. "I like that new song," she said. "I've never heard any jazz before. It's kind of cool."

"Yeah. I like it, too," Jeremy told her. "And . . ."

"Would you two stop talking about band!" Suzanne shouted angrily.

"What's with her?" Jeremy asked Katie.

"She's upset about the Bayside Boys concert," Katie explained. "We don't have tickets, and Becky does."

"I know," Jeremy said. "That's all Becky's talking about. She even wants me to take her test."

"Are you going to do it?" Suzanne asked him.

Jeremy shook his head. "I wouldn't go *anywhere* with Becky."

Katie laughed. Becky had a big crush on Jeremy. But Jeremy didn't like Becky one bit.

"Are *you* going to take the test?" Jeremy asked Suzanne.

Suzanne frowned and kicked at the dirt. "Becky didn't ask me to," she said quietly. "She's only letting certain people take it. She's such a snob."

"Don't worry about Becky," Katie said.

Suzanne sighed. "The only thing I'm worried about is how in the world am I going to get my hands on some tickets!"

X X X

As soon as Katie got home, she raced up to her room. She had to get started on her Aesop project.

Katie liked *Aesop's Fables*. She'd taken the book out of the library because the fables were animal stories. But as Katie had read the stories, she realized there was more to them than just animal tales. They taught important lessons, too. That's what she wanted to talk about in her report.

As Katie opened her notebook, Pepper padded into her room with a new bone in his mouth. He wanted to play.

But Katie didn't have time to play. "Sorry, Pepper. Not now," she told her dog. "I have work to do."

Pepper seemed to understand. He leaped up on Katie's bed and sat there quietly, chomping on his bone.

"Too bad Aesop didn't write a fable about

cocker spaniels," Katie told him as she opened the book to a story called "The Milkmaid and Her Pail." The lesson in that one was:

Don't count your chickens before they hatch.

Katie turned the page. She smiled when she saw the moral of "The Jay and the Peacock." It was a perfect one for Suzanne.

It read:

It is not only fine feathers that make fine birds.

The next story was "The Lion and the Mouse." It was one of Katie's favorites. She liked the lesson in that one:

No act of kindness, no matter how small, is ever wasted.

Katie turned the page to the story of the "Bundle of Sticks." She began to write down that moral, too:

United we stand. Divided we fall.

But before Katie could finish writing the last word, the phone rang.

"Katie, it's for you!" her mother shouted upstairs.

Katie dropped her pencil and raced down to the kitchen to answer the phone. "Hello?"

"It's me," Suzanne said breathlessly. "Turn on your radio."

"Why?"

"Because they're going to have a contest! When Joey G. says to phone in, you're supposed to call the radio station. The one-hundredth caller wins two tickets to the Bayside Boys concert."

"Oh my gosh!" Katie exclaimed. "Suzanne, get off the phone."

"But, Katie . . ."

"Suzanne," Katie repeated firmly. "You *have* to get off the phone."

"Why?"

"Because if you don't, I can't call in to win tickets, and neither can you!"

"Oh. Good point," Suzanne agreed. Then she hung up without even saying good-bye.

Chapter 5

Unfortunately, neither Katie nor Suzanne had any luck winning tickets. Katie had been caller number fifty-three. Suzanne hadn't gotten through to the radio station at all.

In fact, no one in the whole fourth grade—except Becky, of course—had been able to get tickets for the Bayside Boys concert. Lots of kids were complaining about it the next morning as they arrived on the playground.

"I was so sad, all I could do was play the Bayside Boys CD over and over," Emma W. said. "After a while, even the twins were singing along."

"The twins?" Suzanne asked her. "But

they're only two years old."

"Well, they weren't getting the words right," Emma admitted. "But they were trying."

Not everyone was upset at not having tickets, though. George Brennan didn't even like the Bayside Boys.

"I don't know what the big deal is, Katie Kazoo," George said, using the cool nickname he'd given Katie. "The Bayside Boys aren't so great. They don't even play instruments."

"That doesn't mean anything," Katie told him. "They sing really well."

"I think they're lousy. I wish they wouldn't sing at *all*."

"That's mean, George," Katie told him.

"Do you know what you call a band that doesn't make music?" George asked Katie.

"What?"

"A rubber band!" George laughed hard at his own joke.

Suzanne wasn't laughing. "There's nothing

funny about this, George," she told him. She looked over to where Becky was standing a few feet away. She was talking to Mandy.

"The Bayside Boys are coming into town this morning," Becky was saying. "They're staying at the Cherrydale Inn. It's supposed to be a secret. Of course *I* found out, though. That's because I know someone who knows the Bayside Boys."

"What a bragger," Suzanne whispered to Katie. "Don't you just hate people who brag?"

Katie tried hard not to laugh. Suzanne could be a big bragger, too. It's just that right now she had nothing to brag about.

"Wait a minute!" Suzanne exclaimed. "That's it!"

"What's it?" Katie asked.

"We're going to meet the Bayside Boys!"

Katie looked at her friend strangely. "How are we going to do that?"

"Today, after school, we're going to ride our bikes over to the Cherrydale Inn. We'll go to the desk, ask which room they're in, and visit them."

Katie shook her head. "I don't know if I'm allowed to go over to the inn."

"Why not? It's just four blocks from your house. You're allowed to ride your bike four blocks. We do it all the time. You're not breaking any rules."

"I guess," Katie agreed. "But even when we get there, there's *no way* the person at the desk will tell us what room they're staying in."

"Come on, Katie," Suzanne pleaded. "It's worth a try. Just imagine the look on Becky's face when we tell her we met the Bayside Boys!"

Katie shrugged. "I don't want to make her feel bad."

"Okay, then. How about the look on *your* face when you get to shake hands with Spike?"

Now, Katie began to smile. "Well . . ." she said. "It's worth a try."

X X X

That afternoon, Katie and Suzanne hurried to get their bikes. They met at the corner by Katie's house, and pedaled the four blocks to the Cherrydale Inn. When they arrived, the girls parked their bikes and walked into the lobby.

"Okay, let me do the talking," Suzanne whispered to Katie.

Katie nodded. That was fine with her. She didn't like talking to people she didn't know. Besides, the man standing behind the front desk didn't look very friendly.

"May I help you?" he asked the girls as they approached the desk.

"We've got a message for four of your guests," Suzanne told him.

"Which guests?" the man asked.

"They're friends of ours," Suzanne lied. "They're registered under the Bayside Boys."

The man shook his head. "We don't have any guests by that name."

Suzanne frowned. "Well, maybe they signed in under their *real* names. Do you have any rooms for Ace, Fizzy, T-Jon, or Spike?"

"I don't believe so," the man behind the desk replied firmly.

Katie could tell he was getting very annoyed with them. She pulled Suzanne away from the desk and whispered in her ear. "That's it, Suzanne. They're not here. Let's go home."

Suzanne shook her head wildly. "I'm not leaving," she told Katie. "They're here. I know

it. They probably just registered under some fake names so no one would bother them. Remember, Becky said their being here was a secret."

"Let's just go," Katie urged.

But Suzanne wasn't budging. She plopped down on one of the big couches and folded her arms in front of her. "You can go if you want to. But I'm not leaving until I meet a Bayside Boy . . . or until I have to go home for dinner."

"I promised my mom I'd finish my homework early today," Katie told her. "I can't stay here all afternoon . . ."

"*Our* class doesn't have any homework today. Ms. Sweet said it was too pretty a day for us to be inside, working," Suzanne boasted. "She's the nicest teacher."

There was no way Katie could argue that one. She liked Mr. Guthrie a lot. But right now it would have been nice to have been in Ms. Sweet's class. "I gotta go," she said.

"Whatever," Suzanne shrugged. "Just don't

blame me when you miss the chance to meet Spike!"

X X X

Katie's block was very quiet as she pedaled toward home. No one was around. The parents were all at work or making dinner. The kids were inside doing homework. Which was what Katie would have to do as soon as she got home. *Ugh!*

Suddenly, a cool breeze began to blow. Katie shivered a little bit. It was getting kind of chilly. She pedaled faster, so she could get home before it got really cold out.

But Katie couldn't pedal fast enough to beat *this* wind. The breeze blowing on Katie's neck wasn't just any wind. It was the magic wind.

Whoosh! Within seconds, the cool breeze turned into a full-blown tornado. It was whirling just around Katie.

Quickly, she hopped off her bike . . . just before the magic wind knocked it to the

ground. *Phew*. That was close.

Katie shut her eyes tightly and tried hard not to cry. All she'd wanted to do was get home and do her work. But she wasn't going to be able to do that now. The magic wind had seen to that.

Suddenly, the tornado stopped. Everything was calm again.

The magic wind was gone. And so was Katie Carew.

Chapter 6

Katie stood there for a moment, afraid to open her eyes. She had no idea where—*or who*—she was. It was a very scary feeling.

The one thing she knew for sure was that she wasn't outside anymore. The smell of the trees and freshly cut grass on her block were gone. Instead, her nose picked up the scent of air conditioning and soap.

"We're ordering in room service," she heard someone say. "You want anything, T-Jon?"

T-Jon?! Katie's eyes shot open. Was it possible? Could she be in the same room as the Bayside Boys?

It *was* possible. And as Katie looked in the hotel bathroom mirror, she realized she wasn't just *with* the Bayside Boys.

She *was* one of the Bayside Boys. The face that stared back at her from the bathroom mirror had cool round sunglasses and just the slightest touch of a beard on the chin. The magic wind had turned her into T-Jon!

And the other Bayside Boys were right outside that bathroom door. Wow! Katie had to admit that this time the magic wind had done something really cool. She was going to get to meet Ace, Fizzy, and Spike!

"Yo, T-Jon, you want food or not?" someone called into the bathroom.

Slowly, Katie opened the bathroom door. As she stepped into the living room of the hotel suite, she stuck her hand into her pocket. There was nothing inside.

"I . . . um . . . I don't have any money," she said.

Fizzy laughed and put his hand over the

phone. “Yeah, like we need cash. The record company’s picking up the bills now, remember?”

“You’re Fizzy,” Katie squealed excitedly.

Fizzy looked at her strangely. “Yeah. *And* I’m hungry. So order something, will you?”

But Katie was too excited to eat a thing. “Oh my goodness!” she exclaimed. “Spike!”

Spike looked around quickly. “What’s the matter?” he asked nervously.

“Nothing,” Katie assured him. “It’s just that I can’t believe I’m here in the same room with you . . . with *all* of you!”

Ace walked over and draped a long arm around Katie’s shoulder. “T-Jon, dude, are you all right?”

“Yeah, you’re acting kind of strange,” Spike agreed.

“Are you ready to order or not?” Fizzy demanded of Katie.

“No,” Katie quickly replied. “I’m not very hungry.”

"Okay, so that's it," Fizzy said into the phone. "Just have them bring up the food when it's ready." He hung up. "Room service should be here soon," he told the others.

"Okay, how about we work on the new tune while we're waiting for the eats?" Ace suggested. "I still need a little work on that second verse."

"Yeah, and T-Jon hasn't finished his rap for it yet," Spike said. He turned to Katie. "Come on, man, we've got a radio interview tomorrow morning and the first sound check is tomorrow night."

"Which is why we really need to work on this now," Ace agreed.

"Okay," Fizzy agreed. "Let's take it from where I come in with the high part." He opened his mouth and began to sing. "*Wherever I travel . . .*"

Katie couldn't believe her ears. Fizzy didn't sound anything like the way he did on the CD. In fact . . . "That was awful!" she blurted out suddenly.

Fizzy stopped singing and glared in Katie's direction. "Excuse me?" he demanded.

"It just sounded so high and squeaky," Katie told him, scratching the little patch of red hair on her chin. "Are you sure those were the right notes?"

That made Fizzy angry. "What's that supposed to mean?"

"Nothing," Katie said quickly. "I just thought . . ."

"Yeah, well *stop thinking*," Fizzy shouted back.

"Hey, guys, cool it," Ace said. He stepped between them. "How about we take it from *my* vocal?"

"Good idea," Katie said. "You have such a nice voice. My friend Suzanne says it makes her all tingly."

Ace shook his head. "Maybe you better sit down, dude. You're acting all weird."

Katie gulped. She'd been so excited about

being with the Bayside Boys, she'd forgotten she was one of them. She'd have to be careful about what she said.

"Okay. From the top," Ace said. Then he

began to sing. "*When I'm traveling down that highway, with nothing but road ahead . . .*"

"Is that how you're going to sing it on Saturday?" Katie blurted out.

"You know another way?" Ace asked her.

"It's just that it sounds so boring," Katie said. "So plain."

"That's because it's missing the harmonies," Fizzy said. "Oh, wait, that's right. You didn't like my harmonies, either."

Fizzy could be really scary when he was angry. Katie was surprised. He sure never looked that way in the magazine pictures.

"You know what?" Spike interrupted. "We haven't heard anything from T-Jon yet." He looked straight at Katie. "Instead of criticizing everyone else, why don't you show us what you got?"

Uh-oh. He expected her to rap! Right here. Right now. How was she supposed to do that?

Katie gulped. This was *so* not good.

Chapter 7

Katie just sat there for a minute, trying to figure out a way to get out of rapping in front of the Bayside Boys. But she couldn't be quiet forever.

"See, I told you T-Jon hadn't written anything yet!" Fizzy announced to the others. "The guy just can't rap anymore."

Katie scowled. Fizzy was being very mean. "I can too!" she declared angrily. Then she gasped. Why had she said that?

"Prove it, then!" Fizzy demanded. "Let's hear the new rap."

There was only one thing to do. Katie had to rap. "Okay, here goes," she said. "*It's great to be here at the show. Rappin' to people I don't know. I gotta admit it's kind of cool. To be up here instead of sitting in school. I'm tired of homework and teacher's tricks. I'd rather be up here making musics."*

Phew. She'd done it! She'd come up with a rap. And it was a pretty good one, if she did say so herself.

Unfortunately, the other Bayside Boys *didn't* say so. In fact, they hated it!

"*School? Homework?*" Ace asked her. "What does that have to do with anything?"

"This song is about a guy on the road, missing his girlfriend," Spike added. "He's a little old for teachers and homework. Who in the audience is gonna relate to that?"

Katie bit her lip and tried to fight back the tears. She couldn't believe they were being so hard on her.

Suddenly, Ace announced, "I'm not going on stage and making a fool out of myself."

"What are you saying, man?" Spike asked him.

"I'm saying I'm not going to do a show with you guys," Ace snapped. "No one's taking this seriously."

"I am," Spike insisted.

"So am I," Fizzy agreed.

"Fizzy, all you care about is ordering room service, and all the stuff the record label will pay for," Ace argued. "You don't care about the music anymore. Even T-Jon can hear that."

Fizzy looked shocked. "T-Jon can't even rap anymore! Why are you listening to him?"

"Because he's right," Spike interrupted. "You didn't sound so great before."

"Exactly," Ace agreed.

"And neither did you," Spike continued, looking at Ace. "T-Jon wasn't kidding. You did sound boring. And your harmonies *were* totally off."

"Oh, yeah?" Ace shouted. "Well, the *fans* think I'm great. Who do you think they come to see, anyway? *Me*. That's who."

"Hey, that's not true," Spike disagreed.

"I'll prove it," Ace said. "I'm going to record my own CD. I'll bet my solo album sells more copies than the Bayside Boys CD *ever* did."

"I can't listen to this anymore," Fizzy said.

He picked up his jacket. “I’m out of here.” He stormed out of the room.

“Me too,” Spike agreed. “I need a break from you guys.”

“Funny, that’s just what I was thinking,” Ace said, angrily grabbing his jacket and leaving the room just behind his ex-bandmates.

X X X

Katie sat there in the hotel suite, thinking. She was kind of sad. The Bayside Boys were nothing like the magazines said they were. For one thing, they didn’t sound very good. At least not when they sang separately. And they weren’t very nice to one another, either.

Suddenly, Katie felt a familiar breeze on the back of her neck. Within seconds, the breeze began to blow harder . . . and harder . . . and harder, until it was a wild tornado, blowing just around Katie.

The magic wind was back!

Katie shut her eyes tight and pulled her knees to her chest. She held on tight, trying not to get blown away.

And then it stopped. Just like that.

Slowly, Katie opened her eyes and looked around. There was the couch and the TV and the bathroom door. Okay, so she was still in the Bayside Boys' hotel suite.

But she wasn't alone anymore. The *real* T-Jon was right there on the sofa next to her. He seemed really confused.

"Hey, you're not supposed to be here!" T-Jon shouted at Katie. He leaped up from the couch. "No fans are allowed. How did you get past that big guard at the door?"

"I . . . um . . ." Katie didn't know what to say. How could she explain the magic wind to T-Jon?

Knock. Knock. Before Katie could answer, someone came to the door.

"Who's there?" T-Jon asked.

"It's room service." The security guard opened the door and poked his head inside. "Okay to let him in?"

"Awesome!" T-Jon exclaimed. "I'm starving."

As the guard opened the door, Katie ducked behind the couch. She didn't want the guard to catch her there. How could she explain what she was doing in the room?

Katie secretly watched as a waiter entered the room, pushing an elegant cart with a long flowing tablecloth and lots of silver-covered dishes.

T-Jon reached into his pockets. "Oh, sorry, dude," he said to the waiter. "I'm out of cash. But I'll put a nice tip on the bill, okay?"

"Thank you, sir," the waiter said.

"Don't thank me. Thank the record company."

As soon as the security guard and the waiter left, Katie popped up from her hiding place.

T-Jon walked over to the cart and took the silver lid off one of the plates. "Yum. Burger and fries." He turned to Katie. "Did you order this for me?"

Katie shook her head. "I think Fizzy did."

T-Jon shrugged. "Oh. Where is Fizzy, anyway?"

Katie gulped. "He . . . um . . . he went for a walk or something."

"Oh, yeah," T-Jon said, taking a big bite of a hamburger. "I think I remember that. Sort of. I'm not sure what I remember. It's all kind of blurry."

Katie watched as T-Jon ate a huge handful

of french fries. He might have been confused, but it hadn't hurt his appetite.

"I don't even remember meeting you," T-Jon continued, sounding even more curious about what was happening. But he quickly came to his senses. "Whoever you are, you gotta get out of here. And don't tell anyone where we're staying. All we need is a bunch of fans like you storming the place."

Katie frowned. If kids knew the way the Bayside Boys had just sounded, they wouldn't even have any fans.

For a minute, Katie thought about asking T-Jon for an autograph before she left. But she changed her mind. She didn't want to wait around for him to ask her any more questions.

"Bye," she shouted, racing out the door.

"Hey, how'd you get in there?" the guard demanded in a loud, booming voice as she passed by him.

Katie just kept running.

Chapter 8

The next morning, Katie and Suzanne walked to school together. Suzanne was in a really bad mood.

"I waited in that hotel lobby for half an hour," she complained to Katie. "And not one Bayside Boy showed up!"

"Maybe that's a good thing," Katie said slowly.

"How can you say that?!" Suzanne demanded.

"Well, it's just that they're probably nothing like we think they are," Katie said. "What if you met them and you didn't like them?"

"That would never happen," Suzanne assured Katie.

Just then, Emma W. came running onto the playground behind the school. Tears were streaming down her face. "I've just heard the worst news!" she cried to Katie and Suzanne.

"What?" Suzanne asked.

"It's the Bayside Boys," Emma sobbed. "They broke up."

Katie gasped. "Are you sure?"

Emma nodded. "I just heard it on the car radio. The concert is cancelled."

"Did they say why they broke up?" Katie asked.

"No," Emma said. "They just made the announcement."

Becky Stern walked over just as Emma finished speaking. She'd obviously overheard the whole conversation. "*I* know why they broke up," she boasted. "My dad's friend said the guys all want to record their own CDs. They're leaving town on separate airplanes tonight!"

Suzanne started crying, too. "I don't believe it," she said.

But Katie believed it. She knew something about the boys' big fight that even Becky's dad's friend didn't know. The Bayside Boys' breakup was all Katie's fault.

This was soooo not good!

X X X

Katie spent the whole day thinking about the Bayside Boys. She couldn't let them break up. Somebody had to do something . . .

And that somebody was Katie!

But Katie was too shy to talk to the boys all by herself. She needed someone to go with her. Someone who wasn't afraid of anyone. Not even the big security guard who stood at the Bayside Boys' door. She needed someone like . . . Suzanne!

Right after school, Katie raced over to talk to her best friend. "We have to go to the Cherrydale Inn right away!" she told her. "We have to find the Bayside Boys!"

Suzanne shook her head. "I can't go back there today. I have my modeling class in half an hour."

"So what?" Katie demanded. "I have my cooking class. But I'll miss it if it means getting the Bayside Boys back together. What's more important?"

Suzanne thought about that for a minute.

"You have a point," she said.

"Okay, so let's go now," Katie said. "We have to get to their suite and convince them to stay together."

"But we don't even know what suite they're staying in," Suzanne reminded her.

"It's on the eighth floor," Katie told Suzanne.

"How do you know?" Suzanne asked.

"Never mind," Katie told her. "I just know. Now come on!"

X X X

Katie might have known which suite the Bayside Boys were staying in, but that didn't mean she and Suzanne would be able to get inside to talk to them. The big, burly guard was standing outside their room. He wasn't letting anyone in.

"But we just want to ask them to stay together," Katie pleaded with the tall, strong guard.

"You and every other kid in town," the

guard replied. "Look, I don't know how you found out where the Bayside Boys were . . ."

"I was wondering the same thing," Suzanne agreed.

"But they're packing up," the guard continued. "They have to leave in a few minutes. They don't have time to talk to fans. Why don't you two go home?"

"But . . ." Katie began.

"I said, 'Go home!' " the guard shouted.

"Yes, sir," Suzanne said. She ran toward the elevator.

Katie followed right behind her. That guy was scary!

As soon as they got in the elevator, Suzanne pushed the button marked *L* for Lobby. "Let's get out of here," she shuddered.

"But we haven't spoken to the Bayside Boys yet," Katie argued.

"Didn't you hear that guard? We're not *going* to talk to them," Suzanne sighed heavily. "It's all over."

Just then, the elevator door opened up on the third floor. As a man and a woman got on, Katie looked out the open door. A room-service cart was sitting in the hallway.

Suddenly, Katie got another one of her great ideas.

"Come on, Suzanne," she said, pulling her friend out of the elevator. "It's not over yet!"

Chapter 9

"Katie, this is never going to work," Suzanne said a few minutes later. "That guard will never let us past the door. He'll never believe we work at the hotel."

"He won't *know* it's you," Katie said. She pulled a white jacket out from under the cart. It looked like someone had spilled some grape juice all over it. The waiter must have gone to get a clean jacket and left his cart in the hallway. "You'll be wearing this disguise."

Suzanne made a face. "It looks disgusting. I would *never* wear something like that."

"Just put it on," Katie demanded. "This is an emergency, not a fashion show!"

Katie had never ordered Suzanne around before. Suzanne was in such shock, she did what she was told without an argument. Then she looked down at the name tag and shook her head. "It says Tom," she told Katie. "Who's going to believe my name is Tom?"

"Just tuck your ponytail under this hat," Katie said, handing Suzanne the white waiter's cap that had been placed under the cart with the jacket. "And keep your head down, so the guard can't see your face."

"And where will you be through all this?" Suzanne demanded.

Katie lifted up the tablecloth on the cart and crawled underneath. Then she pulled the cloth back down to make sure she was hidden. "I'll be right here the whole time," she assured her friend.

"This will never work," Suzanne sighed as she pushed the elevator button.

X X X

The big guard was talking on his cell phone when Suzanne pushed the cart up to the Bayside Boys' hotel suite. His back was turned away from her. Quickly, she snuck past him and knocked on the door.

"Room service," she shouted loudly.

The guard spun around quickly. "Don't you listen?" he shouted at Suzanne. "I told you to leave before."

"That wasn't me," Suzanne murmured nervously.

"Sure it was, kid. You think I can't tell it's you under that hat?" the guard answered.

Before Suzanne could reply, the door swung open.

"Oh, cool," Fizzy said. "Eats."

"I tried to get rid of her," the guard assured Fizzy. "But . . ."

"Why would you try to get rid of room service?" Fizzy asked. He stepped aside and let Suzanne push the cart inside.

Before the guard could do anything, Fizzy

slammed the door shut. Suzanne's mouth dropped open. The Bayside Boys were all there, in the living room of the suite. She was so shocked, she couldn't even speak.

But Katie sure could. She popped out from beneath the cart. "Hi!" she greeted Ace, Fizzy, Spike, and T-Jon.

"You again?" T-Jon asked.

Ace looked at him strangely. "You know this kid?"

T-Jon nodded. "She was here the other day. You know, when we had the big fight."

"No, she wasn't," Ace told him. "I didn't see her."

"I didn't see her, either," Spike agreed.

T-Jon looked really confused. "But, I . . . she . . . oh, I don't know," he sighed.

"It doesn't matter when T-Jon met me," Katie interrupted. "The important thing is that I'm here *now*. And my friend and I really need to talk to you. We don't think you should break up. Do we, Suzanne?"

Suzanne didn't say anything. She was too busy staring.

"Listen, kid," Ace began.

"Katie," she corrected him.

"Okay, *Katie*. It's time for us to break up. I want a solo career."

"We all do," Spike added.

Katie shook her head. "It won't work," she told them. "When you're singing as the Bayside Boys, you're awesome. But you guys don't sound nearly as good apart as you do together."

"How would *you* know that?" Fizzy asked her. "No one's ever heard us sing apart, except us."

"Then *listen* to yourselves," Katie insisted. She looked straight at Fizzy. "Go ahead. Sing something."

Fizzy smiled. "Prepare to be amazed," he told the girls. He opened his mouth and sang in his high voice.

Suzanne's eyes popped open even wider as

he sang. She made a face. "You don't sound like that!" she blurted out.

"What?" Fizzy asked her.

Spike laughed. "I think she means your voice is too high to make it as a solo singer," he said. "Now *this* is the voice of a star." He began to sing one of his low harmony parts.

Suzanne shook her head again. "That's too low. Most people's voices don't go down that far. How could anyone sing along with you on the radio?"

Now it was Ace's turn to chuckle. "That's why I'm the only one who's going to make it big on his own. I sing lead."

"Yeah, but without us, it's a boring lead," T-Jon said. "Which is why *I'm* the only one who has a shot at making it big on his own. My rhymes are what have made the Bayside Boys stand out."

"That's not true," Katie told him.

T-Jon stared at her angrily. "What do you mean?" he demanded.

"The Bayside Boys are great because your styles all mix together perfectly," Katie explained. "*That's* what makes you special."

"Katie's right," Suzanne agreed. "I wouldn't buy an album by any one of you. But I'd buy a new Bayside Boys CD."

"I wonder how many other girls would agree with her," Spike admitted.

"You're going to listen to a kid?" Ace asked him.

"No," Spike answered quickly. "It's just something to think about, that's all."

"Well, *I'm* not thinking about it," T-Jon told him.

"Me either," Fizzy agreed. "I'm ready to break out on my own."

"Yeah, but if these two girls feel like this . . ." Spike began.

"Oh, please. They're just kids," Ace told him. "They don't know anything."

"Well, if you're not going to listen to a kid, would you listen to a writer?" Katie suggested. "A really *famous* one?"

"What writer?" Ace asked. "Is he a music critic?"

Katie shook her head. "Actually he wrote fables. His name was Aesop. One of his most famous lessons was, 'United we stand, divided we fall.' "

"That's right," Suzanne agreed. "If you guys break up, none of you will ever be really big stars. But as the Bayside Boys . . ."

"As the Bayside Boys we sell out concerts," Ace said, interrupting her. "Whoa." He looked at his bandmates. "Maybe we better think about this some more."

"That's what I was trying to tell you," Spike replied.

"That Aesop was one smart dude," Fizzy added.

T-Jon smiled at Katie. "And *you're* one smart kid. You just saved our careers."

"If there's anything we can do for you," Spike said. "Just tell us."

"Yeah," Fizzy agreed. "We owe you."

"Well . . ." Katie said slowly. "There is one thing you can do."

Chapter 10

"And I dream of you when I awake!" Katie and Suzanne sang out happily. The girls were sitting in the front row of the Cherrydale Arena on Saturday night. Like everyone else in the audience, they were singing along with the Bayside Boys.

"These seats are amazing!" Suzanne squealed as the guys finished the song.

"I think this is the best night of my life!" Katie shouted back.

As the song ended, Ace waved to the audience. "This next song is dedicated to two amazing fans. They taught us that we need to work together in harmony. Let's hope the whole world can learn that lesson. Katie and Suzanne, this is for you! It's our brand-new song, called 'United.' "

Katie couldn't believe her ears. The Bayside Boys had dedicated a song to them, right in front of everyone. This was a dream come true.

Suzanne thought so, too. “I wish I could see the look on Becky’s face now,” she said. “But I can’t. Because she and Jessica are sitting all the way back there.” She turned and pointed toward the back rows.

Katie laughed. Suzanne would be bragging about this for a long time. Some things never changed.

And maybe that was a good thing. Some things *should* stay the same. Like Katie’s favorite band. They were perfect just the way they were.

“Bayside Boys FOREVER!” she shouted.

Katie's Kazoo!

Katie loves music. She listens to the radio all the time, and she loves singing along with her favorite songs. She also plays the clarinet in her school band.

You can make music too! Just try building your own kazoo.

You will need:

a toilet paper roll
contact paper
scissors
waxed paper
a rubber band

This is what you do:

1. Cover the toilet paper roll with the contact paper.
2. Ask an adult to punch three small holes in the roll with the scissors.
3. Cut a small square of waxed paper and fit it tightly over the end of the tube.
4. Use the rubber band to secure the waxed paper to the tube.
5. Now hum into the open end of the tube. *Woohoo!* Listen to you. You're just like Katie Kazoo!

Love Stinks!

by Nancy Krulik • illustrated by John & Wendy

Grosset & Dunlap

For *my* valentine, from your
not-so-secret admirer—N.K.

For Karen—a real sweetheart!—J&W

 Published by Grosset & Dunlap, a division of Penguin Young Readers Group, 345 Hudson Street, New York, New York, 10014. GROSSET & DUNLAP is a trademark of Penguin Random House LLC.
Manufactured in China

Library of Congress Cataloging-in-Publication Data

Krulik, Nancy E.

Love stinks! / by Nancy Krulik ; illustrated by John & Wendy.

p. cm. — (Katie Kazoo, switcheroo ; 15)
Summary: When the magic wind turns fourth-grader Katie, who dislikes the "mushy gushy stuff" of Valentine's Day, into a candy store owner, she decides to write her "love messages" on the candy hearts.
ISBN 0-448-43640-X (pbk.)
[1. Valentine's Day—Fiction. 2. Magic—Fiction. 3. Candy—Fiction.] I. John & Wendy. II. Title. III. Series.

PZ7.K9416Lo 2004
[Fic]—dc22 2004015226

10 9 8 7 6 5 4 3 2 1

Proprietary ISBN 978-1-101-95136-1
Part of Boxed Set, ISBN 978-1-101-95128-6

Chapter 1

"So are you playing goalie at your soccer game today?" Katie Carew asked her best friend Jeremy Fox. They were walking home from school together after band practice on Monday afternoon.

Jeremy didn't answer Katie. Instead he dropped his head and ducked behind her. "Hide me!" he whispered.

"From what?" Katie asked him.

"From *Becky*. She's coming this way."

Everyone in the fourth grade knew that Becky Stern had a crush on Jeremy. Jeremy didn't like Becky at all. But this was the first time he'd ever actually hidden from her.

Katie giggled. “Oh, come on. She’s not that bad.”

“You want to bet?” Jeremy said. “She’s been following me for two weeks! She keeps talking to me about Valentine’s Day.” He ducked down even farther.

Now Katie understood. Valentine’s Day was this Saturday. Becky was probably hoping that Jeremy would be her valentine. Considering Jeremy was *hiding* from Becky, Katie doubted that would ever happen.

Unfortunately, Becky spotted Jeremy behind Katie. “There you are,” she called out to him in her soft Southern accent. “I’ve been looking all over for you.”

“Why?” Jeremy asked her.

“To give you these.” Becky held out a clear plastic bag filled with chocolate kisses. “I saw them at Cinnamon’s Candy Shop and thought of you.”

Jeremy frowned. “No, thanks. I don’t eat candy. I’m in training.”

Katie tried hard not to laugh. That hadn't stopped him before. Just yesterday he'd eaten a whole bag of gumdrops!

But Becky wasn't insulted that Jeremy wouldn't take her gift. In fact, she seemed impressed. "Oh, Jeremy, you've got such willpower," she cooed. "I should be in training for my gymnastics classes, too. We're working on backflips. Look what I learned this week." Becky turned around to make sure no one was coming and flipped in the air, right in the middle of the sidewalk!

"That was really good!" Katie said.

Becky smiled. "Thanks. What did *you* think, Jeremy?"

"It was okay," Jeremy mumbled. His face was redder than Katie's hair! "I . . . um . . . I gotta get going. I've got a soccer game."

"Oh, okay," Becky said. "Well, see ya later . . . Happy almost Valentine's Day!"

Jeremy rolled his eyes and walked off. Katie hurried to catch up to him.

"You see what I mean?" Jeremy asked her.

"I'd say she definitely *flipped* for you!" Katie joked.

Jeremy groaned.

"Don't worry. Valentine's Day will be over soon," Katie told him. "She won't bug you so much after that."

"I hope not," Jeremy said.

"I can't believe you gave up a whole bag of chocolate kisses. They looked delicious."

"It wasn't hard," Jeremy assured her. "I'm still full from yesterday. Can you believe how much candy we ate?"

"I didn't eat that much."

"Only three licorice sticks, a bunch of sour lemon drops, and a rainbow-colored lollipop," Jeremy reminded her.

"Oh, yeah. I forgot about the lollipop," Katie said. She licked her lips. "Cinnamon's Candy Shop has the best lollipops."

Jeremy nodded. "I'm so glad Cinnamon decided to open a candy store in the mall."

Katie knew exactly what he meant. Cinnamon's Candy Shop was located right across from the Book Nook, the store Katie's

mom managed. It was a fun place to hang out while Katie waited for her mom to finish with work. Sometimes Katie brought her friends, like Jeremy and Suzanne Lock, to hang out there with her.

Cinnamon was really nice. She let Katie dip strawberries into dark chocolate or fill the penny candy drawers with bubble gum, hard candies, and tiny chocolate bars. Best of all, she always gave Katie free lemon drops.

"You'd better hope Becky doesn't visit Cinnamon's Candy Shop this week," Katie told Jeremy.

"Why not?"

"Cinnamon is selling giant candy hearts," she explained. "She'll put any message you want right on the heart. Cinnamon guarantees to have the heart delivered in time for Valentine's Day!"

"That would be so embarrassing!" Jeremy exclaimed.

"Well, if Becky does send you a heart, at

least it will be delicious." Katie was trying to make him feel better.

But it didn't work. "I hate Valentine's Day!" Jeremy grumbled.

Chapter 2

But not all the fourth-graders hated Valentine's Day. In fact, Wednesday afternoon, right after her cooking class, Katie hurried over to Suzanne's house. She, Becky, Emma Weber, and Jessica Haynes were all getting together with Suzanne to make valentines for their friends.

"Oh, that's a cute one," Emma said as she looked at the long, thin, squiggly-shaped card Katie was working on. "It looks just like Slinky."

Suzanne looked curiously at Katie. "You made a valentine for a *snake*?"

"Of course," Katie told her. "Animals need

love, too. I even made one for my dog, Pepper."

"Pepper's cute, but Slinky is creepy," Suzanne said with a shudder.

"Slinky is *not* creepy!" Katie insisted.

"I'm glad *our* class has a guinea pig. I love Fuzzy," Suzanne boasted.

Suzanne was always bragging about what was happening in class 4B. But Katie didn't care. She was glad Suzanne was happy in her classroom. Katie was certainly happy in hers.

Class 4A was a very different kind of classroom. Katie had never been in one like it before. Her teacher, Mr. Guthrie, wasn't very strict. He let the kids sit in beanbag chairs instead of at desks. He thought they learned better when they were comfortable.

Mr. Guthrie did other cool stuff, like letting George Brennan and Kadeem Carter have joke-telling contests. He called them joke-offs. And Mr. Guthrie had gotten the class the coolest pet in the whole school—Slinky the snake. The kids had raised him ever since he'd

hatched from his egg.

“Look what I made for Jeremy,” Becky announced, interrupting Katie’s thoughts. She leaped to her feet and held up a giant red construction paper heart with lace trim. “Do you think he’ll like it?”

Katie knew Jeremy would hate getting a huge card from Becky. But she didn't tell her that. Katie didn't like to hurt people's feelings.

"I don't know what you see in Jeremy," Suzanne said. "He's such a jerk."

"That's mean, Suzanne," Katie told her.

Suzanne shrugged. "He's *your* best friend, Katie. Not mine."

Katie nodded. That was the truth. Suzanne and Jeremy were both Katie's best friends. But they didn't always like each other very much.

"Who are you making valentines for, Suzanne?" Jessica asked her.

"Just for my very best friends," she said. "I don't want to waste time making cards for people who aren't going to give *me* one."

"That makes sense," Jessica said. "Oh, and just so you know, I'm making one for you."

Emma W. was busy making her valentines. "Do you have any more pink construction paper?" she asked.

"Sure," Suzanne told her. "It's over there,

next to Heather's play kitchen." She pointed to a little plastic kitchen that was filled with plastic food, pots, and pans.

Heather was Suzanne's one-year-old sister. Lately, Suzanne's whole house had begun to look like a toy store. There were stuffed animals, rag dolls, and big rubber balls all over the place.

Emma certainly didn't mind. She had three younger brothers. She knew what it was like to live with a lot of toys around. She just stepped over the dolls and balls to reach the construction paper. "My twin brothers have the same kitchen," she told Suzanne. "But theirs isn't as nice. It's a hand-me-down."

"That one's brand-new," Suzanne told her. "My parents are always buying new toys for Heather." She sounded a little jealous.

Ding dong. Just then, the doorbell rang.

"I'll get it," Suzanne called out, loud enough for her mother to hear. She leaped up from the table and raced for the door.

When Suzanne returned, she was carrying a big cardboard box in her hand.

"It's a package from Cinnamon's Candy Shop," Suzanne announced. "And it's addressed to me!"

"Oh, yummy," Becky said. "Who sent it?"

"I don't know," Suzanne replied as she looked at the box.

"Is there a card or anything?" Emma W. asked.

"Maybe it's on the inside," Jessica suggested. "Open it."

"Okay, okay, don't rush me!" Suzanne exclaimed excitedly. She carefully began to open the box. "It's one of those giant candy hearts!"

Katie looked down at the sugary pink heart. It looked just like the little pink candy message hearts Cinnamon sold at the store. But this heart was the size of a small cake!

Cinnamon had etched a picture of a bumble bee and the word MINE onto the heart. "Be mine," Katie realized.

"A candy valentine!" Jessica squealed. "Who is it from?"

Suzanne picked up a small white envelope from the bottom of the box. "It says, 'Happy Valentine's Day from your secret admirer.' "

"Wow!" Becky exclaimed. "A secret admirer. I wish I had one of those."

Suzanne laughed. "Come on, Becky. It's no secret who *you'd* like to get candy from."

Becky blushed while all the girls giggled.

All except Katie, that is. She was getting really tired of hearing about how much Becky liked Jeremy. After all, Jeremy was her best friend. And Becky was making him really unhappy.

"So who do you think the admirer is?" Emma asked Suzanne.

"Maybe it's a boy in our class," Jessica suggested.

"It could be an older boy. Like in the *fifth* grade," Emma W. thought out loud.

"I don't know," Suzanne said. "It's a mystery."

"We'll figure out who it is," Jessica assured Suzanne. "Starting tomorrow, we're all going to look around and see if any of the boys are paying special attention to you."

"Maybe he doesn't go to our school," Suzanne quickly suggested.

"Then where would he be from?" Becky asked.

Suzanne said with a shrug, "He could be from anywhere."

Katie rolled her eyes and looked over at her best friend. Suzanne was clearly enjoying all the attention. But she didn't seem as excited by the candy heart as Katie thought she might be.

There was something weird about this whole secret admirer thing. Katie just couldn't figure out what it was.

Chapter 3

First thing Thursday morning, Katie and most of the girls in the fourth grade gathered on the playground. But Katie wasn't happy. All anyone could talk about was Suzanne's secret admirer. Emma, Becky, and Jessica must have been on the phone all night telling people about it. Katie really didn't care about Suzanne's secret admirer.

When Kevin Camilleri walked by, Jessica turned her attention to him.

"Hey, Kevin," Jessica called out. "What do you think of Suzanne?" she asked.

Kevin frowned. "I think she's a snob."

"So you're not her secret admirer?"

"If I am, it's a secret to me!" Kevin ran off to kick a soccer ball with Andrew Epstein.

"We can cross Kevin off our list," Jessica said.

Emma W. nodded. "You can cross George Brennan off, too. I called him last night. He doesn't like Suzanne very much."

"Do you think it could be Jeremy?" Jessica asked Katie. "He's your best friend, so you should know."

Katie shook her head. "I don't think so."

"That's a relief," Becky said.

"I've already talked to Andrew and Kadeem," Emma W. told the girls. "They didn't even know Cinnamon was making big candy hearts. So neither of them could be the secret admirer."

Katie sighed. She really didn't want to talk about this anymore. Katie was tired of hearing about all the mushy, lovey-dovey stuff. She was already sick of Valentine's Day . . . and it hadn't even come yet!

At just that moment, Suzanne strolled onto the playground. She was holding a small white envelope in her hand.

"Hi, everyone," she greeted the crowd of girls.

"Hi, Suzanne," Jessica replied. "We've been talking to all the boys in the fourth grade. So far, we haven't been able to figure out who your secret admirer is."

"Well, maybe this will help," she said, holding out the white envelope. "I found it in my mailbox this morning."

Katie wondered why Suzanne had been looking in her mailbox first thing in the morning. The mail usually didn't get delivered until after they were in school.

Jessica took the envelope from Suzanne. Inside was a note made up of letters that were cut from magazines. It read:

Be Mine.

From,
Your Secret Admirer

“Wow!” Miriam exclaimed.

“That’s so romantic,” Becky added.

“Well, I guess we won’t be able to figure out who he is from his handwriting,” Katie said.

“He’s good at keeping his identity a secret,” Emma W. noted. “I’ll bet he’s really smart.”

"Well, that leaves out any of the fourth-grade boys," Jessica joked. "None of them are very smart."

Just then, the school bell rang. "We're not going to be able to solve this now," Suzanne told the others. "It's time to go inside."

Becky turned just as Jeremy, Kevin, and Manny Gonzalez were walking by.

"Hey, Jeremy," she called.

"Hi, Becky," Jeremy mumbled back.

"Are you going to our cooking club meeting Saturday?" she asked. Every Saturday some of the kids in the fourth grade met at Katie's house to cook. Sometimes they used recipes from Katie's Wednesday after-school cooking class or sometimes they just made their own creations. Either way, it was a lot of fun.

"I've got a soccer game in the morning," he told her. "But I'll probably come after."

"Oh, good, I'm going to the meeting, too. Maybe we can cook a Valentine's Day treat together," Becky said hopefully.

Jeremy blushed.

Katie sighed. It was obvious Becky had made Jeremy uncomfortable . . . again!

But Becky didn't seem to notice. "See you in class," she told him. Then she ran off into the school building with Suzanne and Jessica.

"Oh, Jeremy, that sounds soooo romantic," George teased.

"Yeah," Manny added. He batted his eyelashes wildly. "We can cook together. *Oooo.*"

Katie watched Jeremy's face. She could tell he didn't think George and Manny were very funny.

"I wish there was no such thing as Valentine's Day!" he shouted out angrily.

Katie gasped. Jeremy had just made a wish. That could mean real trouble!

Katie knew that sometimes wishes came true. And not the way you meant them to, either.

Katie's troubles with wishes all started

one day at the beginning of third grade. Katie had lost the football game for her team, ruined her favorite pair of pants, and let out a big burp in front of the whole class. That night, Katie had wished she could be anyone but herself.

There must have been a shooting star overhead when she made that wish, because the very next day the magic wind came.

The magic wind was a wild tornado that blew just around Katie. It was so powerful that every time it came, it turned her into somebody else! Katie never knew when the wind would arrive. But when it did, her whole world was turned upside down . . . *switcheroo*!

The first time the magic wind came, it turned Katie into Speedy, the hamster in her third-grade class! Katie escaped from the hamster cage and wound up in the boys' locker room! Good thing the magic wind turned Katie back into herself before the boys found out a girl had been in there!

The magic wind came back again and again after that. Sometimes it changed Katie into other kids—like Jeremy, Emma W., Becky, and Suzanne. Other times it turned her into adults—like Lucille the lunch lady, Principal Kane, and the school music teacher, Mr. Starkey. That had been an *especially* bad time. The kids in the band definitely did not make beautiful music while Katie was conducting.

That was why Katie didn't make wishes anymore. She didn't want them to come true.

Luckily, Jeremy's wish *hadn't* come true. All of the kids' beanbag chairs were covered with hearts, cupids, and other Valentine's Day decorations.

There would be a Valentine's Day. At least in class 4A.

Chapter 4

"Can I come to the mall with you today after school?" Suzanne asked Katie as the girls left school together at the end of the day. Suzanne knew that Katie often hung out at the mall on Thursdays. That was the day Mrs. Carew worked late at the Book Nook.

"Sure. My mom's picking me up in a few minutes," Katie told her. "Don't you have to ask permission?"

Suzanne nodded. She pulled a small silver phone from her backpack. "My mom said I could borrow her phone today," Suzanne told her. "Just in case I wanted to go home with someone after school."

"I thought cell phones weren't allowed in school," Katie reminded her.

"I kept it hidden in my backpack," Suzanne replied. "No one even knew it was there."

"Hey, what are you guys doing?" Jessica asked as she, Mandy, and Becky walked over.

Suzanne put her finger to her lips. "*Shhh.* I can't hear."

"She's calling her mom to see if she can go to the mall with me," Katie whispered.

"Cool," Jessica said. "Can I come, too?"

Katie nodded. "If your mom says it's okay."

"How about me?" Becky asked.

Katie shrugged. "Sure. And you, too, if you want, Mandy."

"Oh, this will be great!" Becky exclaimed. "When we get to the mall, we can talk to Cinnamon about Suzanne's secret admirer. Since Cinnamon made the heart, she's *got* to know who he is!"

"Do we have to keep talking about Valentine's Day?" Katie asked them.

"What else is there to talk about?" Becky asked her.

Katie sighed. The girls were really making her crazy. She wished she could spend the day with Jeremy. She was sure he wouldn't bring up Valentine's Day once.

As the girls borrowed Suzanne's cell phone to call home, Katie spotted Jeremy, George, Kevin, and Manny walking in the distance. She ran over to them.

"Hey, guys," she said. She turned to Jeremy. "I'm going to the mall. Cinnamon said I could help her put the new lollipops into the display case. Do you want to help?"

Jeremy looked over to where the girls were all gathered around Suzanne and her cell phone.

"Not if *they're* going," he told her, pointing to the girls.

"Why not?"

Before Jeremy could answer, George puckered up his lips really tight. "Oh, Jeremy,

I love you!" he said in a fake Southern accent.

"You're such a *lover boy*," Kevin added.

"Lover boy, I love you," Manny joked.

"That's why I'm not going to the mall," Jeremy groaned. "Cut it out!" he warned the boys.

"We were just joking," George told him.

"It wasn't funny," Jeremy told him. Then he turned to Katie. "I'm not going anywhere near Becky."

"Why don't you go off with the other girls, Katie Kazoo," George said, using the nickname he'd given her. "You can try and figure out who Suzanne's secret admirer is."

"Whoever he is, he's pretty dumb," Kevin said. "Who would want Suzanne for a valentine?"

"Maybe it's Jeremy," Manny suggested. "He's the fourth-grade lover boy." He kissed the air again.

Now Jeremy was really angry. He rolled his hand up into a fist and stared angrily at Manny. "I dare you to say that again," he warned, staring Manny straight in the face.

Katie was surprised. She'd never seen

Jeremy this angry. “Gosh, I’m sorry,” Manny said, quickly stepping back.

“You’d better be,” Jeremy said, walking away. “I’m going home.”

Katie watched as Jeremy stormed off by himself. Valentine’s Day was supposed to be about love. Instead, it was making everyone hate one another.

Valentine’s Day was a real pain!

Chapter 5

"Hi, girls," Cinnamon greeted Katie, Suzanne, Becky, Mandy, and Jessica as they arrived at the candy store later that afternoon.

Katie sniffed at the air. "*Mmm.* It always smells so yummy in here."

"You must be hungry for some candy," Cinnamon teased.

Katie grinned. Cinnamon was just the kind of person who should own a candy store. Her short brown hair was tinted with just a little bit of spicy red, sort of like gingerbread. Her eyes were as blue as blue raspberry lollipops, and her lips were as red as Red Hots.

Most important of all, Cinnamon was a really sweet person.

"Forget the candy," Jessica interrupted. "We have something more important to talk to you about."

"More important than candy? Impossible," Cinnamon joked.

"Seriously," Becky told her. "This is *big*. We have a mystery to solve."

"Oh." Cinnamon sat down on a stool. "It *does* sound important."

"Suzanne has a secret admirer," Becky confided. "And you're the only person who may know who he is."

"Me?" Cinnamon asked. "How would I know?"

"Because he sent her one of your candy

hearts," Mandy explained.

Katie looked over at Suzanne. She was busy looking at the penny candy. She wasn't at all interested in the conversation the girls were having with Cinnamon. That seemed strange to Katie. She would have thought Suzanne would be dying to hear what Cinnamon had to say.

"Can you check your receipts and see who bought that heart?" Jessica asked Cinnamon, interrupting Katie's thoughts.

"I can't do that," Cinnamon told her.

The girls all looked at her, surprised.

Cinnamon shook her head. "I never tell secrets. Especially secrets about secret admirers."

Just then, Suzanne walked over to the group. "I just remembered I have to ask my mother something. I'm going to call her from outside the store. The reception is better outside the shop. I'll be right back."

As Suzanne left the store, the girls all

began picking out penny candy. “Hey, Katie, can you do me a favor?” Cinnamon asked.

“Sure,” Katie replied. “What do you need me to do?”

“Could you go over to Louie’s and get me a slice of pizza?” she asked. “I’m starving.” She handed Katie some dollar bills from her purse.

Katie was amazed that Cinnamon could be hungry with all the candy around! Still, Katie was always willing to do a favor for Cinnamon. “Sure,” she said, taking the money. “I’ll be back in a minute.”

X X X

Louie’s Pizzeria was next to the Book Nook, just across the way from Cinnamon’s Candy Shop. It took Katie only a minute to get there and buy a slice of pizza.

As she walked back toward the candy store, Katie spotted Suzanne. She was hunched down, hiding behind a tall plant. It was pretty obvious she didn’t want anyone

to see her sitting there.

"Operator, I think I'm having trouble with my cell phone," Katie overheard Suzanne whispering into her phone. "I don't think the calls are getting through. Could you please try ringing the phone for me?"

As Suzanne gave the operator her cell phone number, Katie quietly snuck into the candy shop and handed the slice of pizza to Cinnamon.

"Thanks, Katie," Cinnamon said. "You're the best."

A moment later, Suzanne walked back into the store.

"Did you get your mom?" Jessica asked her.

Before Suzanne could answer, her cell phone rang. "Hello?" she answered the phone. Then

her eyes opened wide with surprise. “How did you get this number?”

“Oh my gosh, is it him?” Jessica squealed.

Suzanne nodded but put her finger to her lips to make Jessica be quiet.

“But how did you know I would have a cell phone with me today?” Suzanne asked. Then she giggled. “You are smart.”

“Ask him what his name is,” Becky suggested.

“What’s your name?” Suzanne said into the phone. She listened for a minute. Then she said. “Oh, come on, tell me.”

Katie turned away and frowned. Of course the person on the other end wasn’t going to tell Suzanne his name. That’s because there *wasn’t* any person on the other line. It was just the operator testing the ring on Suzanne’s cell phone.

Now Katie understood why this whole secret admirer thing had seemed so weird. Suzanne didn’t have a secret admirer at all!

She'd made the whole thing up just to get attention. She'd probably even sent herself that candy heart! And the other girls had fallen for the whole thing!

"Suzanne, this is so exciting," Becky cooed as Suzanne hung up the phone. "You know what? I'm going to order a special candy heart for Jeremy. Can I do that now, Cinnamon?"

Cinnamon handed Becky a form. "Just fill this out," she told her. "I'll make sure it's delivered to your valentine by Saturday. Be sure to give me his address."

"Oh, I don't have his address," Becky said. "Can't you deliver it to school?"

"Hmm," said Cinnamon, looking at her watch. "I don't have much time, but if I hurry I can have it delivered to your school tomorrow," Cinnamon answered.

Katie gulped. She knew Jeremy would be really mad if a heart got delivered to him right in front of all his school friends. "No, don't," she warned Becky. But the girls just ignored her!

"I'm going to order a special candy heart, too," Jessica said, taking one of Cinnamon's forms.

"For who?" Suzanne and Becky asked together.

Jessica grinned. "I'm not telling. *I'm* going to be someone's secret admirer."

"That's a good idea," Mandy said. She took a piece of paper from the counter and began scribbling down *her* message. "I know just who to send one to."

"I didn't know you had a crush on anyone," Suzanne told Mandy.

"*Andrew* didn't know it, either. But he will now," Mandy laughed.

Suzanne, Becky, and Jessica all started to giggle.

But not Katie. "This is a bad idea," she warned. "None of the boys will like getting candy at school."

"You're just saying that because you don't have a crush on anyone," Jessica told her.

"And no boy likes her, either," Becky added.

"They do, too," Katie said.

"Sure they do, Katie," Suzanne assured her friend. "But the boys like you as a pal. Not like a *valentine*."

Katie wanted to shout out that no one liked Suzanne like a valentine, either. Her secret admirer was a big fake! But Katie couldn't do that. It would be too mean.

Instead, she turned and walked out of the store. "I'm going back to Louie's for a veggie slice," she told the other girls angrily.

As Katie stormed across the mall, she grew madder and madder. She was sick and tired of Valentine's Day. It was nothing but trouble!

That was it! Katie wasn't celebrating Valentine's Day. She wasn't going to eat any little candy hearts, wear red all day, or make any more cards! As far as Katie was concerned, there was no Valentine's Day. She was calling the whole thing off!

Chapter 6

"Hey there, Katie!" Louie exclaimed cheerfully as she walked into his restaurant. "Back again so soon? Cinnamon must be really hungry."

Katie tried to smile. But it was hard. "This time I'm getting a slice of pizza for myself. My mother gave me five dollars to spend while I'm at the mall." She sighed and plopped onto one of the stools at the counter.

"Bad day, huh?" Louie asked her.

"The worst," Katie agreed. "I hate Valentine's Day."

Louie nodded and ran his finger over his thick, dark mustache. "Ah. So you have a love

problem. Do you have a crush on someone?"

Katie made a face. "Louie! I'm only in fourth grade. I'm too young to be in love."

"I agree," Louie said.

"I wish somebody would tell that to Suzanne, Becky, Mandy, and Jessica though," Katie sighed. "Love is all they talk about these days."

"And that's a bad thing?"

Katie nodded. "*Really* bad. Because of them, Jeremy won't hang out with me. He doesn't want to be near Becky. And some of the other boys are going to be really upset when they find out that they're getting candy hearts at school!"

"They're definitely not going to like that," Louie agreed.

"You wouldn't believe all the weird stuff Suzanne's been doing just because it's Valentine's Day," Katie continued.

"Oh, I don't know," Louie said. "I've seen Suzanne do some pretty odd things."

"Not like this," Katie assured him.

"Well, I know what will cheer you up," Louie told her. "I'll make you a super veggie special—with extra spinach."

Katie looked around. The restaurant was empty. "You're going to make a whole pie, just for me?" she asked him, surprised.

Louie nodded. "You're my favorite customer. You deserve it. Besides, I just had a huge crowd

of college boys in here. They ate all the ready-made pies I had. I've got to make a few new ones. You can help me. I'll let you sprinkle on the cheese."

Katie smiled. Louie always made her feel better.

"Wait here. I'll go in the back and get some more mushrooms and veggies."

"Okay," Katie told him. She sat back in her seat and watched as Louie headed into the back room. She was glad to be alone for a minute. At least she wouldn't have to hear anyone talking about Valentine's Day.

Suddenly, Katie felt a light breeze blowing on the back of her neck. She pulled the collar of her jacket up. But that didn't stop the breeze from blowing on her. In fact, it seemed to get stronger.

Whoosh! Within seconds, the breeze was no longer light and airy. It was more like a powerful burst of wind. A tornado-like wind . . . that was only swirling around Katie.

Katie gulped. This wasn't just any wind. This was the magic wind!

The whirling tornado grew stronger and stronger, blowing around Katie so powerfully that she had to hold her hands over her face to keep her hair from being blown into her eyes. She tensed up her body and tried to keep from being blown away.

And then it stopped. Just like that.

The magic wind was gone.

And so was Katie Carew.

Chapter 7

Katie sat there for a minute, afraid to open her eyes. She sniffed at the air. *Mmm.* Something smelled good.

It wasn't a tangy pizza smell, though. It was sweeter and richer . . . like chocolate.

Slowly, Katie opened her eyes and looked around. She was surrounded by vats of warm melted chocolate, fresh strawberries, and boxes of candy. Katie was in the tiny kitchen in the back of Cinnamon's Candy Shop.

Okay, so that explained *where* she was. But it didn't explain *who* she was.

"Cinnamon," Katie heard Suzanne's voice coming from the front of the store.

"Cinnamon, where are you?" Suzanne called again. Her voice got louder as she came into the kitchen. "Oh, there you are."

Katie looked around. Cinnamon wasn't in the back room.

Or was she? As Katie looked down, she could see she was wearing Cinnamon's cheery red-and-white checkered apron over a pair of cherry red pants. The green nail polish Katie had been wearing was gone. Instead, her fingernails were coated with traces of chocolate.

Katie had turned into Cinnamon!

"Are you okay?" Suzanne asked her.

Katie gulped. She was definitely *not* okay. She didn't want to be Cinnamon. Not right now. Not when she was supposed to be making Valentine's Day candies!

"Cinnamon?" Suzanne repeated.

"Yes?" Katie answered finally.

Suzanne handed Katie three sheets of paper and fifteen dollars. "Here are their

order forms and the money from Jessica, Mandy, and Becky. We're going to go now. My mom's picking us up."

Katie was surprised. "I thought you were going home with my . . . I mean *Katie's* mom," she told Suzanne. *Whoops. That was close.*

"Her mom doesn't leave work until seven o'clock, and Becky, Jessica, and Mandy don't have any money left to spend. If they can't shop, we may as well leave," Suzanne explained. "Besides, we're going back to my house to talk about our crushes. Katie wouldn't want to do that."

That made Katie mad. Suzanne was her best friend. And she was leaving her out of everything!

"Yeah, well, I'm glad you're going," Katie said angrily.

"What?" Suzanne asked.

Oops. Katie gulped. The real Cinnamon never would have gotten mad at Suzanne. "I mean, as soon as you leave, I can make those

hearts. I've got to hurry. The mail carrier will be here soon."

X X X

The minute the girls left the candy shop, Katie locked the door and turned the sign on the door so it read CLOSED. She didn't want to have to pretend to be Cinnamon for all the store's customers.

Then she plopped down on the floor near the penny candy bins and frowned. Everything had gone wrong today. And to top it all off, the magic wind had come and turned her into Cinnamon!

Hmmm. Katie thought about that for a minute. Actually, being Cinnamon wasn't all bad. At least she could eat as much candy as she wanted. After all, she owned the store.

Katie walked over to the lemon-drop bin, and took a big handful. Next, she decided to munch on jelly beans. *Mmm* . . . the red ones tasted like strawberries. Katie took *two* handfuls of those.

After the jelly beans, Katie popped two Red Hots in her mouth at the same time. YIKES! Those were hotter than she'd thought they would be. Just then, Katie spotted some heart-shaped, chocolate-covered mints on the counter. A cool mint was the perfect thing to soothe a hot mouth. Katie took a handful of those, too . . .

Oooh. Suddenly, Katie didn't feel so good. Her stomach hurt. And she had a headache. It figured. Those stupid *heart-shaped* candies had gotten her sick! Even further proof that there should be no Valentine's Day!

Angrily, Katie grabbed the candy order forms her friends had filled out. "LOVE STINKS!" she shouted as she tore them into little pieces.

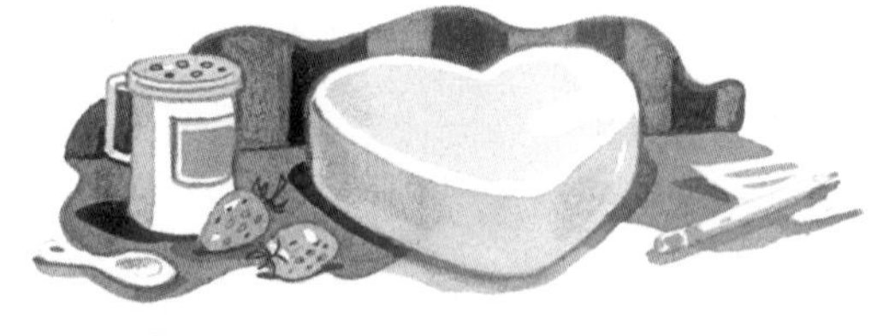

Chapter 8

Katie sat there for a moment, staring at the pile of shredded paper she had just made. She couldn't believe what she'd done! Why did she rip up the forms? She was Cinnamon, and she had to make the hearts! That was bad. Really bad.

Katie looked at the clock. It was 5:15 already and the mailman was coming at 6:00! That didn't leave much time.

She jumped up and raced into the kitchen. She had spotted some of the big candy hearts there on a shelf. Katie grabbed three of them and laid them out on Cinnamon's work area. She picked up the candy chisel from the

counter. She'd seen Cinnamon make the hearts just the other day, when she and Jeremy were at the shop. Chiseling messages hadn't looked so hard then.

The messages! Oh, no! Katie had torn them up. She had no idea what she was supposed to write!

Quickly, she zoomed back into the front of the shop and picked up all the little scraps of paper. Uh-oh. She'd *really* torn them up. It was impossible to make out what words the girls had written.

But Katie was going to have to try. "It's just like a puzzle," she told herself. "All I have to do is put the pieces together."

Eventually, Katie actually managed to put together some messages. But the sentences didn't make a whole lot of sense. At least not to her.

She looked up at the clock. Yikes! There was no more time to figure things out. She'd have to work with what she had.

All she could do was start writing and hope for the best.

Chapter 9

Katie was just putting the last address label on the candy boxes when the mail carrier arrived. He knocked on the door, and Katie let him into the shop.

"Hi, Cinnamon," he greeted her. "Closing early today?"

"I, um, I had to make a lot of candy, so I shut the shop," Katie answered quickly.

"You have any packages for me?"

Katie nodded. "Just these three boxes. They're all going to Cherrydale Elementary School."

"The elementary school!" the mailman exclaimed. "Boy, oh, boy. Don't kids just send

those little paper cards anymore?"

Katie shrugged. "Some do. These girls didn't think that was enough, I guess."

"Kids today," the mail carrier sighed.

"I know," Katie agreed, sounding very much like a grown-up.

"This is a busy time of year for both of us." He patted his mailbag and smiled. "Love is definitely in the air."

Katie rolled her eyes. "Yes, it is," she replied.

"Well, see ya tomorrow," he said as he took the boxes and left the shop.

Katie locked the door behind him and took a deep breath. She was glad she'd managed to get the hearts finished in time. Now all she had to do was clean up the mess she'd made in the kitchen. Katie was not a very neat candy maker. There was sugar everywhere!

But as soon as she walked into the kitchen, Katie felt a slight draft on the back of her neck. She didn't have to look to see if

there was a breeze anywhere else in the shop. She knew there wouldn't be.

The magic wind was back.

And *that* wind only blew around Katie.

The magic wind picked up speed, spinning wildly around her like a full-blown tornado. Katie gripped onto the kitchen counter and shut her eyes tight.

And then the wind stopped. Just like that.

Katie opened her eyes slowly and looked around. She was still in the shop's kitchen. But she wasn't alone anymore. Cinnamon was there, too. She looked very confused.

"What happened here?" Cinnamon asked Katie. "This place is a mess."

"I think you were in a hurry to get those candy hearts finished," Katie told her.

"Candy hearts?"

Katie nodded. "You know the ones that Jessica, Mandy, and Becky ordered?"

"Oh, yeah," Cinnamon said. "I have to make those. Or did I already do that? I'm not

sure. It's all kind of foggy."

"You made them, and you gave them to the mailman," Katie assured her.

Cinnamon shook her head and sat down on a stool. "I think I need to get a breath of fresh air," she said. "I'm going to take a walk."

"Okay," Katie said quickly.

"Do you want me to help clean up?" Katie asked.

"No. I'll straighten the kitchen when I get back. After all, *I* made the mess."

Katie frowned. Not exactly. But she couldn't explain that to Cinnamon. "Okay, bye!" she shouted as she darted out of the store as fast as she could.

Chapter 10

Katie groaned as her alarm clock went off on Friday morning. She was not looking forward to this day. Today, class 4A was celebrating Valentine's Day. And Katie hated Valentine's Day.

"Happy Valentine's Day, sleepyhead," Katie's mom called cheerfully as she walked into Katie's room.

"Grr . . ." Katie pulled the covers over her head.

"I got you an early Valentine's Day gift," her mother said, peeling back the covers and handing Katie a small package.

Katie unwrapped the gift and sighed.

Inside was a package of new tights—white ones with tiny black hearts on them.

"I thought you could wear them to your class party today," Mrs. Carew suggested.

Katie didn't want to disappoint her mother. "Thanks, Mom," she said, forcing a smile.

× × ×

Katie's new tights fit right in with her classroom. On Friday, class 4A was the Valentine's Day capital of the world! Mr. Guthrie had made a giant mobile with all the cards he'd received from his students. It was hanging from the ceiling. Cardboard cupids flew joyously over the blackboard, and red construction paper hearts were plastered to the side of Slinky's glass tank. Katie thought the whole room looked horrible!

And of course, all the kids had decorated their beanbag chairs with the cards they'd given one another. *All the kids except Katie, that is.* Her beanbag wasn't decorated at all.

Katie spent most of the morning watching

MINE
LO
VE
YOU
ROCK

the door to her classroom. The candy hearts would be delivered sometime today. She didn't know when. But she did know that once they were, there would be big trouble.

The boys were already sick of all the girls looking at them and giggling. When they got those candy hearts, they were going to go *crazy*!

But there weren't any special deliveries that morning. By lunchtime, Katie began to relax. Maybe the hearts weren't coming after all. Maybe Katie had gotten something wrong on the address labels. Or maybe the school didn't let kids get mail during the school day, or . . .

No such luck!

As soon as the fourth grade entered the lunchroom, Mrs. Davidson, the school secretary, walked in. She was carrying three big boxes.

"I have special packages," she announced. "Will Jeremy Fox, Andrew Epstein, and Kevin Camilleri come get their mail?"

Katie gulped. This was the moment Katie had been dreading.

Jeremy was the first boy to open his box. "Oh, no, it's a heart," he groaned.

Becky ran over to him. "It says just how I feel."

"Ooooh," the boys teased.

Jeremy read the message on the candy.

"Huh?" Jeremy asked.

"She thinks she can crush you," Kadeem laughed. "That's just wrong, dude."

Katie looked over at Jeremy. He looked furious!

Becky looked down at the heart. "That's not the message I wrote," she insisted. She sounded like she was going to cry.

Andrew was the next to open his box. "Who is this from?" he asked.

"Mandy," Suzanne and Jessica shouted out.

Mandy blushed. Andrew blushed harder as he opened the box.

"Love your what?" Andrew asked her.

Mandy looked at the heart curiously. "That's not right. Cinnamon was *supposed* to write 'Won't You *Be* Mine?' "

"Well, I won't," Andrew told her.

Now it was Kevin's turn.

"Oh, look, it's *another* lover boy!" George squealed, making his voice go up really high.

"Ooh, Kev's got a girlfriend," Manny added.

"Why me?" Kevin moaned. As he opened his box, Kevin looked like he was going to be sick. But when he read the heart, a smile returned to his face.

"I don't have a secret admirer after all," he said as he held up the candy heart. "This isn't for me!"

Kevin turned proudly to the guys. "See, it's for some people named Val and Tim."

"It's not supposed to say that!" Jessica

announced suddenly. "It was supposed to say 'Love, Your Secret Valentine'!"

Oops! Now everyone knew Jessica was Kevin's secret admirer.

"Jessica and Kevin sitting in a tree," George began to sing. "K-I-S-S-I-N-G."

That made Kevin plenty mad. "Stop it, George. Or I'll tell everyone you still sleep with a teddy bear."

That sure made Kadeem laugh. "A teddy bear! What a baby!" he exclaimed.

Now *George* was mad. "You swore you'd never tell," he shouted at Kevin.

"*I'll* tell you something. I'm never going back to that candy store!" Becky announced.

"Me, neither," Mandy agreed.

"I'll never forgive Cinnamon for this," Jessica added.

Katie frowned. *This was so not good.*

Chapter 11

After school, Katie went to the mall with her mother. Mrs. Carew had to stop by the Book Nook to wait for an order of books that was due to arrive.

As they passed by Cinnamon's Candy Shop, Katie got very sad. Usually, the store would be filled with kids buying penny candy. But today there were only adults in there—buying last-minute gifts, Katie guessed.

"Katie!" Cinnamon came running out of the store as Katie and her mom walked by.

"Oh, hi," Katie said quietly.

"Weren't you going to visit me today?" asked Cinnamon.

Katie had been too ashamed of what she had done to visit Cinnamon. "Well, I, uh . . ." she began.

"You know, it's the strangest thing," Cinnamon told Katie and her mother. "None of the fourth-graders have come to the store today. Usually they're here by now."

"That *is* strange," Mrs. Carew agreed. "Your store has become quite a hangout."

"I know. But today, they all just walked by. Some of the girls even looked angry with me."

Now Katie felt *really* bad. "You don't think you'll go out of business, do you?" she asked nervously.

Cinnamon smiled kindly. "No, sweetie. I actually make most of my money from adults who buy chocolate gift boxes. I just *like* having the kids around. That's why I opened a candy store. Kids always come when there's candy around." She paused for a moment. "At least they did until now."

"Do you have any idea what might have

changed?" Mrs. Carew asked.

Cinnamon shook her head. "That's the strange thing."

Katie knew what was wrong. She also knew it was all her fault.

Just then, Katie got one of her great ideas. "You should have a party!" she blurted out.

"A party?" Cinnamon asked.

Katie nodded. "A great big Valentine's Day party. With balloons and music. I'll bet the kids would come to that. I could call all the fourth-graders and invite them."

Cinnamon thought for a moment. "I could give out little bags of candy hearts as favors."

Katie flinched. "I think the kids have had enough of those," she said quickly. "Maybe you

could just give out regular candies."

Cinnamon shrugged. "Okay. I'll do it. I hope this brings the kids back to the store."

So do I, Katie thought to herself.

X X X

"But you *have* to come, Suzanne," Katie begged her best friend. The girls were talking to one another on the phone later that evening. "If you don't, nobody will."

"Well, I *do* set the trends in our grade," Suzanne agreed.

Katie sighed. Suzanne was such a show-off. But she wasn't wrong. Most of the girls *did* copy whatever Suzanne did.

"Still, Cinnamon really messed things up," Suzanne continued.

"Not for you," Katie told her. "Your heart came to your house Wednesday night. It said exactly what it was supposed to."

"I guess," Suzanne agreed. "But . . ."

"Cinnamon probably only made the mistakes since she was rushing. You guys

did have a last-minute order, after all. Cinnamon is a really nice person," Katie said. "She keeps secrets really well."

"What's that supposed to mean?" Suzanne asked.

"She didn't tell anyone about your secret admirer," Katie told her.

"She said she couldn't."

"I know," Katie agreed. "But *I* can tell if I want to."

"Tell what?" Suzanne sounded nervous.

"Who your secret admirer is. I figured it out. But I kept your secret. And so did Cinnamon. You owe us."

Suzanne was quiet for a minute. Katie crossed her fingers. She would never really tell Suzanne's secret, but this was the only plan she had. Katie hoped it would work!

"All right," Suzanne agreed. "I'll come."

Katie was relieved. "And you'll get some of the other girls to come, too?"

"I'll try," Suzanne said slowly.

Katie smiled as she hung up the phone. That took care of the girls. Now she had to deal with the boys.

Quickly, she dialed Jeremy's phone number. When he answered the phone, she told him all about the party.

"I'm not going anywhere near there," he told Katie. "I'm staying as far from Becky as I can."

"I don't think that's too smart," Katie replied.

"Why?"

"Well, look what happened the last time Becky went to Cinnamon's. She got you a heart. At least if you're there, you can make sure she doesn't do anything like that again."

Jeremy was quiet for a moment. Finally, he said, "I guess you're right."

"I know I am," Katie assured him. "We'll go to the party right after our cooking club meeting. It'll be fun, I promise."

Chapter 12

Katie spent the whole evening calling her friends. Her phone calls really worked. Almost everyone in the fourth grade agreed to come to Cinnamon's Valentine's Day party.

The next day, the kids arrived at Cinnamon's Candy Shop. But they didn't look like they were in the mood to party. Instead, they all looked angry. The girls still hadn't forgiven Cinnamon for what was written on their hearts. And the boys hadn't forgiven the girls for sending the hearts in the first place.

Cinnamon wasn't about to let the kids have a bad time. She just kept smiling and handing out candy. Her smiles—and her sweets—were

too much to ignore.

“Wow! Free candy!” Jeremy exclaimed. “Awesome.”

“Can I have some more jelly beans?” George asked Cinnamon.

“Sure,” Cinnamon replied. She handed him a bag of red and white ones. “Eat up.”

"Woohoo!" George exclaimed.

"This is my favorite song," Suzanne said as a Bayside Boys song came on the radio. She started to dance.

So did Jessica. She *always* did whatever Suzanne was doing.

"Admit it. Cinnamon throws a great party," Katie said, dancing over to the girls.

"Yeah, well, she owed it to us after the mess she made," Jessica told Katie.

"But I think we can find it in our *hearts* to forgive her," Suzanne said.

Jessica laughed. "I guess so."

Before long, it seemed as though everyone had put the candy heart mess behind them. They just wanted to have a good time.

But no one was having as good a time as Cinnamon. Seeing her smiling again almost made Katie forget just how much she hated Valentine's Day.

"Come in the back room with me," Cinnamon said as she walked over to put her

arm around Katie. “I have a special surprise.”

“For me?”

Cinnamon nodded. “I think you’ll like it.”

Katie followed Cinnamon back into the kitchen.

“Here you go.” Cinnamon handed Katie a big cardboard box.

Katie smiled as she quickly whipped the top off of the box. Inside was a candy heart that read:

“Valentine’s Day is a nice time to thank your friends for how happy they make you,” Cinnamon explained.

Katie smiled. “I never thought of it that way,” she admitted. “I figured it was just about love and crushes and mushy stuff.”

Cinnamon shook her head. “It doesn’t have

to be." Cinnamon peeked out into the front of the shop. The kids were laughing, talking, and snacking on candy. "See, no one's acting mushy out there."

"Do you think this whole *crush* thing is over?" Katie asked hopefully.

"For now," Cinnamon told her.

That was going to have to be good enough. "In that case, I have to leave for a few minutes," Katie said suddenly.

"Leave? Why?"

"I have to get to the pet shop. I didn't get Pepper a valentine this year. And he's my very best friend. Maybe they have a heart-shaped liver treat for him."

Cinnamon made a face. "*Liver?* Yuck. I'm glad I make treats for *people*."

Katie laughed.

"Happy Valentine's Day," Cinnamon said as Katie turned to leave.

"Happy Valentine's Day," Katie answered. And she really meant it.

A Card Idea from Katie Kazoo to You!

Are you puzzled about what kind of Valentine's Day card to send to *your* friends? This jigsaw-puzzle card is a great way to give a piece of your heart.

You will need:
A sheet of thick cardboard
A photo of you and your friend together
Markers
Glue
Scissors
An envelope

Here's what you do:

1. Glue the photograph of you and your friend onto the piece of cardboard.

2. Use the markers to decorate the rest of the cardboard. Don't forget to write your name!

3. Cut the cardboard into jigsaw puzzle pieces. Make them all different shapes and sizes.

4. Place the puzzle pieces into an envelope and give them to your friend. Your pal is sure to have a fun time putting the card together!